The Ala

Other '*Be A Detective Mystery Stories*'
available in Armada

NANCY DREW® AND THE HARDY BOYS®
Be A Detective Mystery Stories™

The Alaskan Mystery

Carolyn Keene and
Franklin W. Dixon

Illustrated by Paul Frame

Armada

First published in the U.S.A.
in 1985 by Wanderer Books,
a division of Simon & Schuster, Inc.
First published in the U.K. in Armada
in 1986 by Fontana Paperbacks,
8 Grafton Street, London W1X 3LA.

Armada is an imprint of
Fontana Paperbacks, part of
the Collins Publishing Group.

Made and printed in Great Britain by
William Collins Sons & Co. Ltd, Glasgow

Dear Fans,

Since so many of you have written to us saying how much you want to be detectives like Nancy Drew and The Hardy Boys, we figured out a way. Of course, we had to put our heads together to create mysteries that were so baffling they needed help from everyone, including Nancy, Frank, Joe, and you!

In these exciting new BE A DETECTIVE MYSTERY STORIES, you'll be part of a great team of amateur sleuths following clues and wily suspects. At every turn, you'll have a chance to pick a different trail filled with adventure that may lead to danger, surprise, or an amazing discovery!

The choices are all yours—see how many there are and have fun!

C.K. and F.W.D.

"We're almost there!" Nancy Drew exclaimed as she looked out the plane window at the city of Anchorage, Alaska. The young detective turned her sparkling blue eyes back to Frank and Joe Hardy who sat in the seats next to her.

"Thanks for letting us in on this case, Nancy," dark-haired Frank said. "I've always wanted to see more of Alaska."

"I'm glad to have your help," Nancy told him, turning her head toward the window again. The sunlight glinted off her titian hair as she gazed down at the beautiful, rugged landscape. "Alaska is a big place to look for a missing person like Rick," she added.

"Rick Jason used to work for the River Heights *News,* didn't he?" asked Joe, the younger of the two brothers.

"Right," Nancy answered. "Then he took a job as a reporter on an Anchorage paper. We were out of touch for several months until I received that strange letter from him."

"What tipped you off that Rick was in trouble?" Frank asked as the plane began its descent.

Turn to page 2.

"He mentioned a secret lead he was working on," Nancy explained. "It involved someone who was playing for high stakes up here in Alaska."

"How long has Rick been missing?" Joe inquired.

"His chief at the paper told me that Rick hasn't shown up for work for three days," Nancy replied.

"Let's go to the newspaper office right after we land," Frank said, checking his watch. "There might be a clue in his desk."

Nancy nodded. "Rick's boss is expecting us."

Just then, the plane wheels hit the runway.

"Looks like we made it," Joe said with a grin.

Forty minutes later, the young amateur detectives walked into the newsroom of Anchorage's largest daily newspaper. Telephones were ringing shrilly and reporters were hunched over the green screens of their computer terminals.

The trio headed for a glass-walled office that had "Editor-in-Chief" lettered on its door. A husky man with a pencil behind his ear got up from the desk inside and greeted them.

"I'm Matt Jenkins," he said, shaking their hands. "You must be Rick's friends."

Turn to page 3.

Nancy nodded and made introductions.

"Rick told me all about you, Miss Drew," Mr. Jenkins said. "He told me you'd make a great investigative reporter."

"Right now, I'll settle for being a good amateur detective," Nancy answered with a smile. "I think Rick may need help."

"I notified the police that he's missing," the editor explained. "But so far they haven't found a trace of him."

"We'd like to look through his desk," Frank announced, "if it's all right with you."

"Go ahead," Mr. Jenkins agreed. "A lead may turn up."

The editor led Nancy, Frank, and Joe outside into the newsroom and stopped beside an empty desk. Nancy slipped into the chair behind it while Frank and Joe began to look through several file folders on top.

"Good luck," the chief said as he turned back to his office. "I've got a paper to get out today."

"Not much here," Nancy said as she pulled open the desk drawers, which contained mostly blank paper, envelopes, and sundry office supplies.

Turn to page 5.

"Let's check out his computer files," Frank suggested. "That's how reporters work now."

"You're right," Nancy agreed. "I see a code number right here. I'll punch it in."

Frank and Joe watched as the girl detective flicked on the terminal and typed in the number. Lines of print immediately flashed on the screen.

"I'll read through the entries Rick made the day before he disappeared," Nancy said, quickly skimming the print on the CRT.

"I found an address book," Frank announced. "This could come in handy later. It probably contains the names of Rick's contacts."

Just then, the telephone rang. Joe picked it up. Before he could say anything, a sinister voice came over the line.

"Keep off the Pribilof Islands until the seal kill is over," a man threatened, "if you want to go on breathing!" Then there was a loud click as the caller hung up.

"Wow!" Joe exclaimed as he replaced the receiver. "I just got a scare call meant for Rick." He told Frank and Nancy what the caller had said.

Turn to page 6.

"The seal kill . . ." Frank said thoughtfully. "I wonder. . . ."

Nancy continued reading the computer screen intently while listening to Frank and Joe. Suddenly, she let out a gasp.

"I think I've found something!" she exclaimed. "Read the last lines of Rick's final entry."

Frank moved closer to the CRT. "Dateline: Fairbanks," he read. "Title: Will Alaska Be Ready for its Next Boom? Confidential sources in Fairbanks have revealed. . . ."

"And that's all," Joe added. "The rest is a mystery, just like Rick's disappearance."

"But now we have some clues to work on," Frank said with excitement. "That telephone threat about the seals could lead us to Rick."

"Or we could go to Fairbanks," Nancy suggested, "and find out what he had discovered. Frank has his address book. We could check out all Rick's contacts in that town."

If you think Nancy and the Hardys should follow their lead to the Pribilof Islands, turn to page 7.
If you think they should go to Fairbanks to investigate Rick's last story, turn to page 12.

"A seal kill sounds like trouble," Joe declared.

"Maybe Rick found out that an illegal hunt is going on," Nancy suggested. "He always had a nose for trouble."

A young woman with black hair and brown eyes passed by the desk and watched them suspiciously.

"Are you friends of Rick's?" she asked.

"I am," Nancy replied, then introduced herself and the Hardys.

"I'm Rose Tutiakoff," the attractive young woman said. "Rick and I were working on a number of stories together."

"Do you know anything about the seals on the Pribilof Islands?" Frank asked eagerly.

"Of course, I'm a native Aleut," Rose answered. "Rick was very interested in the seals. He had several contacts on the island. I think he might have been onto a big story . . . but he was very secretive about it."

"This sounds like a good lead to Rick's disappearance," Nancy mused. Then she asked Rose, "How would we get to the seal islands?"

Turn to page 8.

"Rick asked me that himself just last week," Rose answered. "Reeve Airways flies out to them from Anchorage by way of the Aleutian Islands."

"Thanks for your help," Nancy said, getting up from the desk. "We'd better find out when the next flight is leaving."

"Just a minute," Rose said as the three detectives began to walk out of the newsroom. "There's something I want to give you. Rick asked me to keep it for him. But he never explained why."

Nancy, Frank, and Joe waited while the reporter went to her desk. She returned with a strange-looking carved mask.

"Rick brought this mask back from his last trip to the Aleutian Islands. He told me it was very important. Perhaps you should take it along. It may help you find him."

Nancy took the mask and tucked it into her spacious shoulder bag. She smiled at Rose and said, "Thanks again. We'll keep in touch."

Turn to page 9.

Before leaving the news office, Nancy called the airport and learned that a Reeve Airways flight to the Pribilof Islands would be leaving later that afternoon. While the three friends rode to the airport in a taxi, Joe studied a map of Alaska.

"I just found the Pribilof Islands," he announced after a moment. "They're in the middle of the Bering Sea!"

"Sounds cold!" Frank shuddered.

Turn to page 10.

"At least it's spring and not winter," Nancy appeased him, grinning.

Frank checked his watch as the taxi driver wove through the busy traffic of Anchorage. "The flight takes off in an hour," he said worriedly. "I hope we catch it. There won't be another one for a couple of days."

Forty-five minutes later, Nancy, Frank, and Joe climbed aboard the plane bound for the Pribilof Islands by way of the Aleutian Islands.

Once the craft was airborne, Nancy pulled the mask Rose Tutiakoff had given her from her shoulder bag.

"This must have been made by a native Aleut," she guessed. "I wonder why Rick thought it was so important."

"Don't look now," Joe whispered from her side, "but that man in the seat across the aisle from you seemed shocked when he saw the mask."

Turn to page 11.

Nancy slipped the artifact back into her bag and then glanced casually at the passenger Joe had mentioned.

His eyes shifted nervously away when she looked at him, but a moment later, his gaze seemed drawn back to her bag that held the mysterious mask.

Turn to page 32.

"Rick's story about Fairbanks sounds pretty hot," Frank said. "Let's ask Matt Jenkins about it."

"Okay," Joe agreed. "We can tell him about the telephone threat, too."

Nancy switched off Rick's terminal, and the three sleuths headed back to the editor's office. Matt Jenkins looked up from some news copy as they walked inside.

"Any leads?" he asked, sticking his pencil back behind his ear.

"I picked up a strange call that came in on Rick's line," Joe explained. "A man warned Rick to stay off the seal islands."

A grin broke out over the editor's face as Joe was talking. "You can ignore that lead," he said wryly. "That crank has called up every reporter in the office. We suspect he's a seal hunter who doesn't want any bad publicity."

"Well, that leaves us with the Fairbanks story," Nancy put in. "We checked out Rick's computer file. His last entry was datelined Fairbanks, and the headline was about Alaska's next boom."

"Fairbanks," Matt Jenkins murmured to himself. "I know Rick has some sources there."

Turn to page 13.

"We've got his address book," Frank said. "Maybe we should go to Fairbanks and question the people he's got listed here."

"Good idea," the editor agreed. Then he quickly added, "I just remembered that Rick was renting a cabin near the Denali National Monument. He liked to go there on weekends. Since it's halfway between here and Fairbanks, you might want to check it out. I'll give you the address."

As the editor wrote down the cabin's address, Nancy studied the map of Alaska on his wall.

"I've got a great idea," she announced. "Let's rent a private plane at the airport here. We can go anywhere we want that way. And we'll save a lot of time."

"Terrific," Frank said. "Did you bring your pilot's license? We don't have ours."

"I have mine," Nancy replied.

Turn to page 16.

"I think it would be smart to check out Rick's place on the way," Frank said. "If there's no sign of him, we can still get to Fairbanks by tonight."

Nancy radioed their destination to the control tower and then waited for instructions for take-off. A short time later, the blue and white Cessna lifted off the airfield into the clear, azure expanse of Alaskan sky.

"Hey," Frank called out from the back seat after the plane had leveled off at several thousand feet. "We're going to get a great view of Mount McKinley, the highest peak in North America. Rick's cabin is just southeast of it."

"What spectacular country," Joe exclaimed as they headed north from Anchorage. He gazed down at the blue Susitna River that wound through a forested valley.

"Look ahead to the left," Nancy said. "There's McKinley!"

The majestic snow-capped peak jutted up from a range of mountains to the northwest.

An hour later, Nancy touched down in a smooth landing at an airfield near the Denali National Monument that surrounded Mount McKinley.

"Someday I'd like to climb that mountain," Joe said eagerly, as the three walked away from their plane.

Turn to page 15.

"We have enough adventure ahead of us without climbing Mount McKinley," Nancy said with a laugh. "Rick's cabin is in the wilderness five miles from here."

In a building near the airfield, the three sleuths made arrangements to rent a Land-Rover to drive to Rick's isolated cabin.

"I'm in the driver's seat this time," Frank announced as they climbed into the rugged jeep. "This'll be as much fun as flying."

"It's a good thing we brought along our hiking clothes," Nancy said, glancing at the heavy wool jackets and sturdy boots they were wearing. "This is rough country around here."

"You've got the map, Joe," Frank asked as he switched on the engine.

"Right, brother," Joe said. "Head up north!"

Turn to page 27.

Several hours later, Nancy, Frank, and Joe walked onto the Anchorage airfield toward the Cessna four-seater they had just rented.

"It's a nice-looking plane," Nancy said, her blue eyes sparkling with excitement. "I can't wait to take it up."

"Who do you want as your navigator?" Joe asked eagerly.

"You can sit up in front with me," Nancy answered. A moment later, the three young detectives climbed aboard the Cessna and Nancy checked out the plane's equipment.

"Everything appears to be in good shape," she reported to Frank and Joe. "I'll have to radio our destination to the control tower before take-off. What do you think we should do? Go on to Fairbanks or make a stop-over at an airfield near Rick's cabin?"

*If you think Nancy should fly straight to Fairbanks,
turn to page 17.
If you think the detectives should stop at Rick's cabin,
turn to page 14.*

"Rick's story about Fairbanks seemed too good to miss," Frank said. "My bet is that he went up there to check out his leads."

Joe nodded in agreement.

Nancy radioed her destination to the control tower and received instructions for take-off. Soon, the blue and white plane was lifting off into the clear Alaskan sky.

"Wow, look at that country!" Joe said enthusiastically a minute later as he gazed at the mountainous terrain below.

"How's our fuel supply, Nancy?" Frank asked jokingly. "I wouldn't want to make an emergency landing here."

"The tank's full," she answered with a smile. "We'll be in Fairbanks in about an hour."

"That place was a boom town during the gold rush of the early 1900s," Frank said. "Now it's booming again because of the oil pipeline."

"I wonder what kind of boom Rick's story was going to be about?" Joe asked.

"I don't know," Nancy mused. "But I hope it hasn't blown up in his face. He may have taken on more than he could handle."

Turn to page 18.

During the flight, Frank carefully examined Rick's address book for the names of people the reporter knew in Fairbanks. By the time Nancy landed the Cessna at the airport, Frank had a list ready.

"Let's get settled in somewhere and have dinner," Nancy suggested after they had left the plane. "Then we can start looking up Rick's contacts."

Two hours later, after a big meal of Alaskan salmon and home fries, Nancy, Frank, and Joe walked out onto the dusky streets of Fairbanks. Neon signs blinked over the city's restaurants and entertainment spots.

Frank checked the street signs until he found the first one he was looking for.

"This is Glen Avenue where Lyle Cooper lives. His name is underlined in Rick's book."

The three sleuths turned into the street. It was lined with old apartment houses.

"This is it," Frank said, pointing to a red brick, four-story building.

The young detectives went up to the door. A large woman came out just then.

"Lyle Cooper?" she said in response to Frank's inquiry. "He is working on the pipeline near Livengood. Lyle's a boomer, you know."

"A boomer?" Nancy questioned.

"That's what we call a person who came up from the lower forty-eight to work on the pipeline," the talkative woman explained.

Turn to page 19.

She went on to tell them that someone fitting Rick's description had visited Lyle at his apartment several times recently.

"Thanks for your help ma'am," Frank said.

"What now?" Joe asked as the three walked back to the street. "Lyle Cooper could be a lead to Rick's whereabouts, but perhaps we should check out the other people while we're here."

"Let's try Lisa Crawford on Center Street," Frank suggested with a grin. "Rick had *her* name circled in red."

"She doesn't live far from here," Joe said, consulting his street map.

Fifteen minutes later, an attractive brunette answered Nancy's knock on her door.

"Hi," Nancy began. "We're friends of Rick Jason."

Lisa's deep blue eyes softened at the mention of the reporter's name. "I've been worried about Rick," she said. "He was supposed to call me a few days ago, and I haven't been able to reach him anywhere."

Nancy told Lisa about the young man's disappearance, then asked, "Do you have any idea what story Rick was writing about Fairbanks?"

Turn to page 21.

"Well," Lisa began, "I know about two exclusives Rick was working on. One had to do with the pipeline. His source was living here in Fairbanks."

"Lyle Cooper?" Frank questioned.

"Right." Lisa paused a moment, then went on. "Rick picked up the other story from an old prospector named Jake he met in a restaurant one night. Jake was panning for gold north of a town called Wiseman near the Brooks Range. That's all I can tell you."

"Thanks, Lisa," Nancy said. "You've been a big help. And when we find Rick, we'll tell him to phone you."

"Good luck," the young woman called out as the three detectives walked away.

"We have to get a good night's sleep," Frank decided as they headed back to their hotel, "so we can start out early tomorrow."

Turn to page 22.

"But where should we go?" Joe asked. "We could head north to Livengood to check out the pipeline story."

"Or we could go farther on to Wiseman," Nancy added. "Maybe another gold rush is on!"

If you think the sleuths should pursue the pipeline story, turn to page 29.

If you think they should check out the gold prospector's story, turn to page 38.

"Let's face it, Frank," Joe announced after he had looked into another window of the cabin. "Nobody seems to be here. We'd better get on our way so we make it to Fairbanks tonight."

"All right," Frank agreed reluctantly. "Let's go, then. I sure enjoyed the ride here, anyway."

Nancy, Frank, and Joe climbed back into the Land-Rover. Frank turned around and headed down the road back to the airfield.

"We'll find Rick yet," Nancy said with determination. "I'm not giving up!

Go back to page 17.

"We can't take the chance of following that thief!" Nancy said with determination. "Our flight leaves in less than an hour, and if we miss it, we may never find Rick."

Frank nervously checked his watch, then looked at the plane. "I guess you're right, Nancy. We should go to the Pribilof Islands!"

A short time later, Nancy, Frank, and Joe were flying northwest across the Bering Sea.

"First, we should check out the hotels to see if Rick is registered in one," Joe suggested.

"Good idea," Frank agreed.

"The island we will land on is pretty small," Nancy said, studying a map. "Somebody must have seen Rick. . . ."

"If he ever made it there," Joe added.

Several hours later, the plane began its descent onto the small piece of land surrounded by a cold, choppy sea.

"What are those spots on the beach?" Joe asked as the three detectives peered down at the rugged shore-line.

"They're seals!" Frank exclaimed. "Thousands and thousands of seals!"

Turn to page 25.

"The Pribilofs are one of the main breeding grounds for those fur seals," Frank explained. "They're the islands' biggest attraction."

When they had landed, the young detectives hurried to a telephone in the terminal to book a hotel for the night.

Frank reserved two rooms, then said, "Let's get settled and then inquire about Rick."

Night had fallen over the remote island by the time the sleuths came out of their hotel after dinner.

"Let's walk down to the water," Nancy suggested. "Maybe we'll meet someone who knows about Rick."

"I certainly didn't get any information out of that hotel clerk," Frank muttered.

The three went quietly down to the docks of the old fishing port. The chilly wind that cut through their jackets reminded them of how far north they had traveled.

When they reached the shadow of a warehouse near an old pier, they suddenly heard the sound of voices from a docked boat.

Turn to page 26.

Frank grabbed Nancy and Joe's arms and pulled them deeper into the dark shadow of the building.

"Shh!" he said in an excited whisper.

Turn to page 52.

Frank took the road that led into the forested foothills surrounding Mount McKinley. Joe directed him from the map, on which an employee at the car rental agency had marked the location of Rick's cabin.

"Take a deep breath of this air!" Nancy exclaimed as she tossed her titian hair in the breeze that blew through the open Land-Rover.

"It smells great!" Joe replied from the back seat. "I can see why people come up here to get away from pollution."

Nearly one hour later, Frank turned the Land-Rover onto the small road that led to the cabin.

"Hey, there's a green pickup truck in that stand of trees," Joe pointed out.

"We still have half a mile to go to Rick's cabin," Frank said, driving on. "It probably belongs to somebody else."

Within a few minutes, the three sleuths pulled up to a small log cabin surrounded by birch trees.

"It looks deserted," Frank observed and shut off the engine.

Nancy hopped out of the jeep and strolled up to the door. She knocked several times and waited for an answer as Frank and Joe joined her. After several minutes of silence, Joe tried the door. It did not budge.

Turn to page 28.

"The place seems to be closed up," he said, peering into a window.

"Maybe we'd better head back to the airport and fly on to Fairbanks," Nancy suggested.

"I don't know . . ." Frank murmured. "We drove all the way up here. Maybe we should hang around for awhile."

If you think Nancy and the Hardys should go back to the airport, turn to page 23.
If you think they should investigate the cabin more, turn to page 35.

The next morning, after a huge breakfast of bacon, eggs, and wheat cakes, Nancy, Frank, and Joe took a taxi back to the Fairbanks airport.

"We're all agreed on flying to Livengood, right?" Nancy asked the Hardys as the three buckled themselves into the seats of the rented Cessna.

Frank nodded. "You know, the oil pipeline has caused a lot of controversy in Alaska. Rick might have discovered something really big!"

"I sure hope so," Nancy said as she taxied onto the runway for takeoff. "I know how Rick loves a good story."

Turn to page 30.

The blue and white plane soared into the sky, heading northwest to the small town of Livengood near the Trans-Alaska pipeline.

"There's the pipeline," Joe said a short time after they were airborne. "According to my map, it runs from Prudhoe Bay on the north coast to Valdez on the southern end."

"The oil line has brought a lot of money and jobs to Alaska," Frank said. "But conservationists hate what it's doing to the environment."

"It *is* pretty ugly," Nancy commented, glancing at the scar in the landscape made by the structure.

A short time later, she brought the Cessna down on the small airstrip used by mail planes and other private craft. After landing, the three sleuths hitched a ride to town in a brown van. Nancy asked the driver, a man named Dan Perkins, if he knew a pipeline worker named Lyle Cooper.

"Cooper?" he asked. "I don't recall him. Are you sure he was working around here?"

"That's what his landlady in Fairbanks told us," Joe replied.

"I'm afraid you made this trip for nothing," the driver insisted. "I know all the workers, and I've never heard of any Lyle Cooper."

Turn to page 31.

"The landlady might have been wrong," Frank said. "Maybe we should go back to the plane and fly up to where the old prospector is."

"I could drive you back if you want," Dan Perkins offered eagerly.

"I don't know . . ." Nancy murmured. "Maybe we should stick around for awhile and ask a few questions."

If you think the sleuths should go back to the airport,
turn to page 71.
If you think they should stay in Livengood, turn to
page 40.

"I'm not letting this bag out of my sight," Nancy whispered to Joe. "That man is acting very suspiciously!"

Frank, who was sitting next to the window, whistled softly. "Look at that awesome scenery down there!" he said.

Joe and Nancy leaned over to the small window to see the Aleutian Islands scattered like a chain off the mainland.

"This is the Alaska I wanted to see," Frank went on. "Anchorage was pretty tame compared to this!"

"I wonder where Rick is," Nancy murmured as she gazed at the mountainous islands, "and what kind of trouble he's in!"

An hour later, the plane touched down at Cold Bay, which was in the middle of the chain.

"We have a little time here," Joe said as they taxied to a stop. "There's an hour layover before we fly to the Pribilof Islands. Let's get off the plane."

Nancy nodded. "I'm becoming more and more curious about that mask," she said in a low voice. "Maybe we can find somebody here who knows where it came from."

Turn to page 33.

"Good idea," Frank agreed.

As the three detectives walked to the exit of the aircraft, Joe noticed that the stranger across the aisle was deplaning as well. A moment later, they stepped down onto the small airfield.

"Wow, we're in the middle of nowhere!" Frank said as he looked around.

"Let's go into the terminal," Nancy suggested nervously, gesturing toward the wooden building a short distance away.

As she lifted her hand to point, she felt a sharp tug on her shoulder. Before she could react, the suspicious man from the plane had grabbed her shoulder bag and was running with it toward a car at the side of the airfield.

"He's got the mask!" the girl yelled.

The three sleuths raced after the man, but he jumped into the waiting car. The driver obviously had been waiting for him with the engine idling, and took off before the sleuths could reach them.

Turn to page 34.

"I've got the license number," Nancy said breathlessly.

"We have to get a taxi and follow him!" Joe urged.

"But if we do," Frank announced, "we could miss our flight to the seal islands!"

If you want the detectives to follow the thief with the mask, turn to page 44.
If you think they should stay and fly on to the seal islands, turn to page 24.

Joe moved around to the side of the cabin and peered in another window.

"Come over here!" he called out a moment later.

Nancy and Frank joined him and pressed their faces against the glass. Inside they saw a small kitchen with food laid out on a table.

"Somebody's been in this cabin recently, that's for sure!" Frank said.

Just then, the three sleuths heard the cracking of dry sticks on the forest floor behind them. They whirled around and saw a young man with reddish-blond hair running toward them.

"Rick!" Nancy exclaimed.

"Nancy Drew!" the young man gasped, panting heavily. "Please, can you get me out of here? Three guys are right behind me!"

"Our Land-Rover is over there." Frank pointed. Get in quick!"

Rick followed Nancy and the Hardys to the jeep and all four jumped inside. Frank coaxed the engine to life, just as three burly men emerged from the woods.

Turn to page 36.

"Here they come!" Rick said in a worried voice. "Let's go!"

Frank reversed, then shifted into a forward gear. The Land-Rover took off down the road seconds before the three men reached it.

"Was that a close call!" Rick gasped as he slumped exhausted in the back seat.

"What kind of trouble are you in, Rick?" Nancy asked after she had introduced the Hardys.

Rick reached into the pocket of his heavy, red-and-black plaid jacket and pulled out a small cassette tape.

"I have evidence that could send those guys to jail and cause a scandal in the state government," he explained. "They work for a timber company that was bribing a senator to lobby for the use of federal land."

"But why did you disappear?" Joe questioned.

"When the timber company found out I had this tape, they ransacked my apartment in Anchorage," Rick went on. "I got scared, so I came up here to lay low for awhile."

"Only they found out about your cabin," Nancy added.

"Right," Rick answered. "But, thanks to you, I'm safe now."

Turn to page 37.

"We flew into an airport about forty miles from here," Nancy explained. "That's where we're headed now."

Frank, who had been driving cautiously along the narrow, bumpy road, suddenly let out a low whistle.

"Uh-oh!" he said, looking in the rearview mirror. "Look who's behind us."

The young people turned and saw the green pickup truck they had passed earlier tearing down the road toward them at a dangerous speed.

"I hope everybody is buckled up," Frank said. "We have a wild ride ahead of us!"

Turn to page 53.

The next morning, the three sleuths flew north in the rented Cessna. Nancy was in the pilot's seat, calculating her flight plan to the small isolated town of Wiseman.

"It's just south of the timber line," she told the Hardys. "About fifty miles north of there the land is tundra. Some hardy plants grow on it, but no trees."

"We'll be close to where the Eskimos live," Joe remarked.

"That's right," Nancy confirmed. "Hunting for Rick is taking us far into the interior of Alaska."

The titian-haired sleuth turned her attention to the plane's controls, while Frank and Joe gazed at the wilderness below. Occasionally, they caught sight of the Trans-Alaska pipeline that cut through the land like a gash in the earth.

Several hours later, Nancy sighted a runway near Wiseman.

"I have to be careful," she murmured. "This airfield isn't big enough to allow for miscalculations."

Frank and Joe held their breath as Nancy brought the plane down in a bumpy landing on the seldom used airstrip.

Turn to page 39.

After taxiing to a stop, the young pilot looked over at Joe's white face.

"I know I'm not a bush pilot," she said with a laugh, "but I did pretty well, didn't I?"

"I'm just glad to be on the ground," Joe said with a sigh of relief as he jumped from the plane.

"Oh well, it looks like there's no welcoming party," Frank added as he joined his brother on the empty airstrip.

"I guess we'll have to hoof it into town," Joe said, searching the wilderness around the strip.

"I'm ready," Nancy replied when she had finished checking out the plane. "Let's go."

Turn to page 47.

Frank and Joe agreed with their friend.

"You can drop us off in town, Mr. Perkins," Frank said to the driver. "I think we'll stay awhile and do our own checking on Lyle Cooper."

The young detective noticed that the man's face was set in a scowl.

"All right, do as you please," Perkins commented as he continued toward Livengood. "Just remember, people around here don't like snoopers."

A short while later, Nancy and the Hardys climbed out of the van, thanking Perkins for the ride. He did not reply. As soon as they had closed the door, he roared away, leaving a cloud of dust in their faces.

"There's a little hotel," Nancy said. "I'll go in and ask about Lyle Cooper and Rick."

Frank was still staring after the brown van as it sped up a road to the west.

"I've got a hunch," he said, "that Mr. Perkins knows a lot more than he's telling us. I think Joe and I should try to get a car and follow him."

If you want to follow Nancy into the hotel, turn to page 55.
If you want to follow Frank and Joe, turn to page 41.

"There's a garage across the way," Joe pointed out. "Maybe they have one we could rent."

"Good idea," Frank agreed.

At the garage, the Hardys rented an old Dodge the owner was willing to let go for the day. In response to their inquiries, he also told them that Dan Perkins was an inspector for the pipeline. "His office is in a little building a few miles west of here," he added.

"I hope this jalopy doesn't break down," Frank muttered as he shifted the car into first gear and headed onto the road Dan Perkins had taken.

Twenty minutes later, they spotted the pipeline and the small building the garage owner had told them about. Frank pulled the Dodge into a stand of trees where it would be hidden from sight.

"Let's sneak up and have a look," he suggested. "We might find out what Perkins was trying to hide from us."

As he and Joe crept through the trees toward the inspector's office, they saw the brown van pulling away from the building.

"We'd better follow him!" Joe exclaimed.

Turn to page 43.

"No, I think we'd better stick around," Frank said. "This is a good opportunity for us to inspect his office!"

If you think the detectives should follow Dan Perkins,
turn to page 86.
If you think they should investigate his office, turn to
page 92.

"I think we should go after that guy!" Joe said with determination. "The mask might be connected to Rick's disappearance."

"Look, there's a taxi," Nancy exclaimed, pointing to a battered old car parked near the terminal.

The three sleuths rushed to the cab and asked the driver to follow the thief's car. The man grinned and told them to get in the back.

"We don't get much excitement around here," he said as he pulled away from the terminal. "I don't mind a little chase at all."

"I can see the car up ahead," Frank said, leaning forward to peer through the front windshield. "It just turned right at that fork in the road."

"He'd be going along the coast road then," the driver said. He turned to follow the thief's car and drove into a foggy mist that shrouded the coastline.

"Who lives along here?" Joe questioned, looking at the rocky landscape that bordered the gray sea.

"Fishermen, sea-going folk," the driver muttered, watching the road carefully as the fog increased.

Turn to page 45.

The three sleuths peered out the windows at the lonely houses they passed.

"Stop!" Nancy suddenly exclaimed as the taxi drove up a hill above the craggy coast. The driver braked to a stop, and she pointed to a house with several small out-buildings below them.

"There's the car!" she said. "Let's get out and walk from here."

Frank paid the driver, and the three climbed from the cab into the damp, misty air.

"Wish we had our own wheels," Joe muttered as the taxi drove away.

"We can always get back to the airport," Frank replied. "It's only a couple of miles. Right now, we have to find out what's going on down there."

The detectives avoided the dirt road that led to the buildings and instead crept along the rocks and through the trees. The gathering fog provided cover as they approached the cluster of buildings.

Turn to page 46.

"I'm going to investigate the one behind the main house," Nancy whispered.

"Okay," Frank replied. "We'll sneak up to the house and look in the windows."

If you want to follow Nancy, turn to page 49.
If you want to follow Frank and Joe, turn to page 57.

A short while later, the three young detectives walked into Wiseman, an old mining town that was now just a collection of small cabins.

"Spring is the lively season around here," Frank joked as they walked through the desolate place. "I'm glad it's not winter."

"Let's try knocking on a few doors," Nancy suggested. "Someone has to be here."

At the third cabin, they met a rugged-looking old man with a gray beard.

"You up here to find gold?" he asked the visitors, surveying the Hardys and Nancy curiously. "If you are, you got some hard work ahead of you."

"We're looking for a friend of ours," Nancy answered. "A reporter named Rick Jason. We think he came up here to see a prospector named Jake."

"Does this Jason have reddish-blond hair?" the old man asked.

"That's right," Nancy replied eagerly. "Have you seen him?"

"Sure did. Two days ago he came here asking about Jake. I sent him to Jake's camp on a creek northwest of here."

"How can we get there?" Joe asked.

Turn to page 48.

"Well, you could take a canoe . . . that's what that Jason friend of yours did. But I'd suggest you hike. It might take longer, but you wouldn't have to worry about the rapids in the river. They can be dangerous this time of year."

"Could you draw us a map?" Frank inquired politely. "We've never been here before."

"Figured that," the old man said with a grin and got a pen and paper from his cabin.

Twenty minutes later, Nancy and the Hardys stood by the river that flowed near Wiseman. A canoe rested along the shore, just as the old man had told them. But he had warned them again that hiking to Jake's camp would be a safer bet.

"It's good to know we're hot on Rick's trail," Nancy said. "But how should we follow him . . . on foot or by canoe?"

If you think they should follow the old man's advice and hike, turn to page 68.
If you think they should take the canoe, turn to page 80.

Nancy walked away from Frank and Joe toward the small building at the back of the house. It looked like a storage shed, and had a small window. Cautiously, the young sleuth peered inside.

"Rick!" she gasped when she saw her reporter friend tied to a chair. She looked for any sign of a guard, but the young man seemed to be alone. Nancy crept to the door and turned the rusty knob. To her relief, the door pushed open.

"Nancy!" Rick Jason exclaimed, his blue eyes wide open in amazement as she walked into the room. "How did . . ."

"There's no time for explanations now," Nancy whispered. "Let's get out of here!"

The pretty sleuth took a rusty sickle from the wall and used it to cut Rick's bonds. The reporter rubbed his stiff, sore ankles and wrists, then followed Nancy out of the shed.

"Frank and Joe Hardy are with me," Nancy told him as they approached the house. "Rose Tutiakoff gave us a mask of yours when we set off to find you, but it was stolen at the airport. We chased the crook and followed him here."

Turn to page 50.

"That mask was a clever imitation of the authentic article made here on the islands centuries ago by the Aleutian natives," Rick explained. "The people in that house are art forgers. They sell the fakes to collectors in the States as real Indian artifacts."

"Then the man who stole your mask must have been staking out your office and followed us, assuming that we were working with you," Nancy reasoned. "When he saw we had the mask, he grabbed it."

"I'm glad he did," Rick said. "Who knows what they would have done if you hadn't rescued me."

Just then, Frank and Joe appeared around the side of the house. They gaped when they saw Nancy and her companion.

"I found Rick," the girl said and introduced everyone, then quickly explained about the forgery ring.

Joe glanced into a car that was parked nearby.

"Here's the ride we need to escape," he said in a low voice. "Those guys were so sure of themselves that they left the key in the ignition!"

Frank quickly slipped behind the wheel. Nancy sat beside him while Rick and Joe climbed into the back. A moment later, they roared away from the house.

Turn to page 51.

Nancy glanced out of the rear window. "Hurry, they heard us!" she warned. "Here they come!"

"They'll never catch us on foot," Frank declared.

"I just hope the police will find them after we report them," Joe added.

"What made you come to Cold Bay?" Rick inquired on the way to headquarters.

"We were headed to the Pribilofs," Joe replied. "I picked up a phone call at your office. Someone warned you to stay away from the seal islands until after the seal kill. I still don't know what that was all about."

A wide grin broke out on the reporter's face. "You must have talked to my archenemy, a guy who hunts seals. He hates the stories I write because killing seals is such a controversial subject, even though it is legal at a certain time of the year to reduce the herds."

"Well, he helped you without knowing it," Nancy said with a smile. "We set out for the Pribilofs, but when the mask was stolen at the airport here, we followed the thief and found you."

Joe chuckled. "Your archenemy may have saved your life—and helped us to crack a forgery ring!"

END

Nancy and Joe listened with wide eyes as the name "Rick Jason" floated up from the boat, where two men were talking to each other.

"I can't hear what they're saying!" Frank muttered in frustration.

"The lighthouse!" Joe whispered. "I'm sure they mentioned that right after Rick's name. I saw the lighthouse when we landed today."

"I want to creep up closer to that boat!" Frank decided. "I bet those guys know where Rick is! Come on, Nancy."

"Be careful," Joe warned worriedly. "I'm going to check out the lighthouse. They could be holding Rick prisoner there."

If you want to go on the boat with Frank and Nancy, turn to page 60.

If you want to follow Joe to the lighthouse, turn to page 72.

Frank accelerated as the green pickup began to close the distance between them.

"Those guys are going way over the speed limit," he muttered as he clutched the steering wheel.

"There's a dirt road ahead," Rick told him. "It's a shortcut to the airport, but I'm not sure if it's clear."

"Do you think we should risk taking it?" Frank called back.

If you think Frank should turn off onto the shortcut, turn to page 62.
If you think he had better stay on the main road, turn to page 66.

From page 76.

Nancy hurried away from the Hardys in the direction of Jake's camp. A short time later, she came up to a tattered old tent pitched along the creek.

She glanced quickly around and then opened the flap to peer inside.

"Rick!" she gasped as she saw the young reporter tied up beside a similarly tied gray-bearded man.

"Nancy!" Rick exclaimed. "Am I glad to see you! You're just the person we need. Two thieves are trying to steal Jake's gold that he panned out of this claim. We tried to stop them, but as you can see, we didn't have much luck."

"I saw them downstream," Nancy said as she freed the young reporter and the prospector. "Frank and Joe Hardy came to Alaska with me to find you. They stopped to talk to the two men."

"We'd better hurry to see what's going on," Rick said, pulling Jake to his feet. "Those guys are pretty rough!"

The pretty detective led the way to where she had left the Hardys. As they came up to the spot, she breathed a sigh of relief. Frank and Joe were stretched out exhausted on the bank, but the other two men were lying on the grass, knocked unconscious.

"I found Rick and Jake," Nancy said with a grin. "And I see you've taken care of those thieves!"

Turn to page 104.

Nancy left Frank and Joe and walked toward the clapboard building that advertised rooms for rent. She opened the screen door and walked into a pleasant lobby. She tapped the small silver bell sitting on the long wooden counter at her left.

"Yes, young lady, what can I do for you?" an elderly man with a kind smile asked as he came out of his office.

"I'm looking for a friend of mine," Nancy explained. "His name is Rick Jason."

"Mr. Jason, of course," the manager said. "He's in room 12."

Nancy's blue eyes flickered in surprise at the man's answer. She hadn't expected to find Rick so easily. Just then, she received an even bigger surprise as she spotted Rick coming down the stairs!

"Nancy!" the reporter exclaimed.

"Rick," Nancy cried out. "I thought you were in some kind of trouble. Why did you drop out of sight?"

Rick was about to answer when two men appeared on the steps behind them. The young reporter motioned for Nancy to follow him out onto the broad front porch of the hotel.

Turn to page 56.

"I was just on my way to the police station!" Rick whispered excitedly. "I finally have the information I need to stop those two men in there. Lyle Cooper tipped me off about a rumor that the pipeline was going to be sabotaged. The men you saw and another terrorist named Perkins have been hired to dynamite it. A foreign government is behind it."

"But why didn't you tell your chief at the paper?" Nancy asked.

"I wanted to stay on the story myself," Rick explained. "I was afraid he'd send up a more experienced reporter."

"When do they plan the attack?" Nancy inquired, casting a glance into the lobby where the two men were talking.

"Tonight!" Rick said. "I overheard their plans from my room next to theirs."

"The police have to be told right away," Nancy said. "Let's hurry!"

"Right. My jeep is over there."

Turn to page 112.

"I don't like this, Frank," Joe said nervously as they came around the side of the house. "We don't know how many thugs might be inside."

"Sh sh!" Frank whispered and pointed to the front door, which was slowly being pushed open.

The brothers quickly retreated to the side for cover. But as they did, they ran right into the path of a burly, bearded man who had come up behind them!

"Stop right there!" he ordered, pulling out a knife. A moment later, another man came from the front and grabbed Joe by the arm. He was the thief who had stolen the mask from Nancy. The bearded man jabbed his knife toward Frank. "Get inside," he snarled, "and move it!"

The Hardys exchanged worried glances, then walked into the house and found themselves in a large room. In the middle of it stood a worktable covered with carved masks and plastic bags containing multi-colored stones.

"Jewels!" Joe said under his breath.

"This seems to be a big week for snoopers," the bearded man growled. "Get into the bedroom with that other fool who came around here."

Turn to page 59.

Frank and Joe were roughly shoved into an adjoining room where they saw a young man tied to a bedpost. He watched them curiously as they, too, were tied up.

"We'll deal with the three of you later," the thief threatened. Then he turned to his partner. "Let's get this shipment ready. Then we'll get out of this place."

As the door was slammed shut, Frank whispered to the young man beside him on the floor. "Are you Rick Jason?"

"Yes, I am!" Rick was amazed. "How on earth did you know?"

"Our friend Nancy Drew told us about you," Joe explained. "As a matter of fact, she's outside right now. And she's our only hope for escape!"

Turn to page 77.

"Rick might be in that boat!" Nancy pressed. "Let's go!"

The sleuths crept toward the large fishing vessel that creaked in its moorings on the pier. They could no longer hear the voices of the two men who had disappeared from the deck into the hold of the ship.

"Let's go aboard," Frank whispered. "It's the only way we'll know if Rick is here or not."

"But what if we're seen?" Nancy asked. "Maybe we should notify the police first."

As they hesitated, the moonlight was blotted out by a bank of clouds.

"Now we have good cover," Frank said. "Come on, let's not waste any more time."

Nancy followed him across the short gangway from the pier onto the boat. The sleuths crept quietly across the deck, their jogging shoes padding softly against the wooden planks.

"Hey, here's an entrance to the hold," Frank whispered suddenly. "Let's go."

Turn to page 61.

Nancy held her breath as Frank cautiously lifted the hatch. They saw narrow wooden steps that led down into a dimly lit room.

"Hurry up," Frank urged as he swung onto the stairs.

Turn to page 78.

"Let's try it," Joe urged. "This jeep has a better chance in rough terrain than their pickup."

"Okay," Frank agreed, gripping the steering wheel tightly. "Here we go."

The Land-Rover veered to the left and lurched over the bumpy path that cut through dense forest.

"They're following us!" Nancy called out as she saw the pickup turn onto the shortcut behind them.

"Trouble ahead," Joe called out to his brother. "We're going to get a mud bath pretty soon."

Frank braked in front of a mucky quagmire that stretched across their path for several yards. Then he shifted the jeep into its lowest gear and pulled forward.

"The wheels are spinning!" he muttered worriedly.

"Come on, come on," Joe urged the jeep.

Slowly, the Land-Rover began to creep forward through the deep mud. Frank gritted his teeth and gently pushed down on the accelerator. Several minutes later, they were clear of the mud.

"We made it!" Nancy sighed with relief.

Turn to page 63.

Joe turned around to watch the green pickup as it started to follow them through the quagmire.

A moment later, he yelled gleefully, "Thank goodness they didn't have the power to get through."

"All right!" Frank said happily. "I just hope we'll get out of here ourselves."

Fifteen minutes later, he pulled the mud-splattered jeep onto the road to the airport.

"We're going to make it to Anchorage in time for the morning edition!" Rick exclaimed.

"Always the reporter!" Nancy chuckled, her blue eyes twinkling at her old friend. "But before we leave, we need to do something else!"

"What's that?" Rick asked.

"Call the police and have those criminals dragged out of the mud and taken to jail!"

Rick grinned. "Always the detective," he said.

END

"Those two are probably prospectors themselves," Joe said. "Maybe they're Jake's friends. Let's ask them where he is."

"Okay," Frank replied. "But be ready for trouble!"

Joe led the way upstream to where the two men were examining the contents of their pans.

"Whoopee!" one of them yelled as the sleuths approached cautiously. "Look at this nugget, Sam. It must be worth a couple of hundred!"

Just then, the man called Sam glanced up and saw the Hardys standing near them.

"We got company, Pete," he growled.

Joe cleared his throat. "We're trying to find an old prospector named Jake," he said. "We were told his camp was nearby."

The two men exchanged glances, then got to their feet. They began to walk slowly through the water to where the Hardys stood.

"Who'd you say you were looking for? Sam asked.

Turn to page 65.

Just as Joe was about to answer, Pete lunged forward and threw him to the ground. Sam tackled Frank at the same time, and the two plunged into the creek.

The young detectives quickly recovered and began to defend themselves. Their attackers were bigger than they were, but the Hardys were quicker and better fighters.

Joe caught his opponent off guard with a karate kick. Pete sank to the ground, momentarily stunned. Meanwhile, Frank wrestled with Sam in the water. Finally, he subdued the man and dragged him up onto the grass.

The brothers slumped down on the bank, exhausted. Suddenly, Frank raised his head.

"Here comes Nancy!" he exclaimed, "with two men. They must be Rick and Jake."

Frank and Joe watched as the pretty detective rushed up to them with a worried look on her face.

"Are you all right?" she asked in a concerned voice.

Turn to page 104.

"I don't know, but there it is," Rick said, pointing to a narrow, rutted path off to the left.

Frank hesitated for a moment, and then drove straight on. "No way," he said. "Did you see that tree lying across that road farther up? We couldn't have driven over it. It must have fallen during a recent storm and hasn't been removed yet."

"I saw it, too," Joe said. "What now?"

Frank stared anxiously into the rearview mirror, watching their pursuers draw nearer. "Hold on tight," he said. "I have an idea."

He continued at the same speed. Finally the pickup was right behind them. Frank pulled the jeep slightly to the right to let the truck pull up beside them. Then he muttered through clenched teeth, "Wish me luck!"

He slammed the accelerator to the floor and swung quickly to the left, almost grazing the truck's right front fender. The pickup driver momentarily lost control, and with its brakes screeching, the green truck slid off the road and crashed into a tree.

Frank braked to a halt about fifty yards down the road.

"Why are we stopping?" Rick asked worriedly.

"To see if anybody is injured," Frank answered.

Turn to page 67.

Nancy was looking out the rear window. "No, all three of them just climbed out of the truck! Let's move!"

Frank shifted gears and took off down the road, accompanied by Joe's and Rick's relieved cheers.

"We'll alert the police as soon as we reach the airport," Nancy declared. "They should be able to get here in time to arrest those guys."

"And when we get back to Anchorage," Rick added with a broad grin, "my story will make the headlines!"

END

"Let's play it safe," Nancy said, looking at the map the man had drawn. "We should be able to hike to Jake's camp in two hours."

"Okay," Frank agreed, picking up the backpack they had brought from Fairbanks.

"We have to walk along the river until we come to a small creek on the left. Then we follow that to the next stream, which branches off to the right."

The three sleuths began their trek to the old prospector's mining site. They had to push their way through brush and swat at mosquitoes buzzing about their faces.

"I'm glad we wore hiking boots!" Nancy exclaimed. "This is rough going."

"The old sourdoughs who came up here years ago to pan for gold must have been pretty tough," Frank replied. "But they had gold fever pushing them on."

Turn to page 75.

"Since gold is involved, we'd better check out Jake's camp first," Joe said.

"Right," Frank agreed. "We'll head far into the woods so we won't be seen."

The three sleuths moved away from the stream into the cover of the forest. They walked about a quarter of a mile until they spied a tattered tent pitched by the side of the creek.

"I don't see anybody around," Nancy murmured. "Maybe Rick and Jake are inside."

She led the way to the back of the large, old camp tent. The men who were panning in the water downstream were hidden by a curve in the bank.

"Rick?" Nancy called out expectantly.

A muffled grunt came from inside. The girl threw a worried look at Frank and Joe and then opened the flap of the tent. Two figures were lying on the ground, gagged and tied up.

"Rick!" Nancy exclaimed, rushing over to them.

With Frank and Joe's help, she immediately went to free her friend and an older, gray-bearded man.

Turn to page 70.

The young, blue-eyed reporter stared at her in amazement.

"What are you doing here in the middle of Alaska, Nancy?" he gasped.

"I flew up with Frank and Joe Hardy to find you," Nancy explained. "Lisa Crawford in Fairbanks tipped us off that you might be here with Jake."

Rick's companion groaned as he picked his sore body off the ground. "That's me," he confirmed. "Those thieves downstream are stealing my gold nuggets. I've been saving them up for over a year." Then he added proudly, "I found myself a good claim at last!"

"It's not quite the gold boom you told me it was, though," Rick said.

"Where is the gold you already panned out?" Joe asked.

"Over there," the prospector replied, "in that canvas sack."

"Then let's take it and get out of here," Frank urged. "We can go back to Wiseman and send the police after those crooks."

"Good idea!" Rick agreed. "Come on, Jake, your gold will be safe, and you can come back to pan for more later."

Turn to page 82.

"You know, we could waste a lot of time here looking for the mysterious Lyle Cooper," Joe commented from the back seat. "We have another lead to work on. Why don't we return to the airstrip?"

"All right," Nancy agreed reluctantly. "Mr. Perkins, could you take us back to our plane?"

"Sure thing," Dan Perkins answered as he braked his van to a stop and then wheeled it around.

"Don't worry, Nancy," Frank said as he noticed the anxious expression on the blonde sleuth's face. "We were bound to hit a couple of dead ends."

"I guess you're right," Nancy replied. "I just hope we find Rick before it's too late!"

Go back to page 38.

"An old lighthouse would be a perfect place to hide somebody," Joe whispered. He hurried away from the dock toward the abandoned structure standing half a mile north on the island's coast.

"It sure feels lonely around here," Joe said to himself as he scrambled across the rocky beach. A short time later, he arrived at the round tower and circled its base until he found a wooden door.

"This place looks so deserted," he mumbled. "I'll bet there isn't even a ghost inside!"

Just then, a bright flash of light beamed from the top of the lighthouse.

"Wow!" Joe whispered, "I guess I was wrong about that!"

The beam of light shut off as abruptly as it had come on.

Suddenly, Joe wished he weren't alone. But at that moment, he peered down the beach and saw two dark figures approaching the lighthouse. He recognized them as his brother and Nancy.

"Did you see that light?" Joe asked as he ran up to the two detectives.

"It might have been a signal," Nancy speculated.

Turn to page 73.

"To a boat out on the water," Frank added.

"What happened back at the dock?" Joe asked.

"We didn't discover a thing!" Frank said. "The two men went under deck for the night. Nancy and I searched the boat as best we could but didn't turn up any clues."

"Let's try to get inside that lighthouse," Nancy suggested. "Something odd is going on."

The three sleuths crept up to the door. Frank used all his strength trying to open it, but it was obviously bolted on the inside.

"What'll we do now?" Nancy asked.

"There's an open window," Joe said, pointing to a dark rectangle about twenty feet off the ground. "I bet I could climb up to it. These rough stones have good footholds."

Turn to page 74.

"Too dangerous, Joe," Frank decided. "We can hide out here and wait for somebody to come out."

"That might take all night!" Joe objected. "I'd rather get in through that window."

If you think Joe should try to climb up to the lighthouse window, turn to page 83.
If you think the sleuths should wait for someone to come out of the lighthouse, turn to page 89.

Two hours later, Nancy and the Hardys were still following the small stream that wound toward Jake's camp. They had fallen silent and were looking forward to eating the food they had brought along.

Suddenly, Joe, who was in the lead, stopped in his tracks and held up his hand.

Frank and Nancy followed his gaze upstream to where two men were stooped over, gazing intently into the perforated pans they held.

"Neither of them is Rick," Nancy whispered. "And neither looks old enough to be the prospector Jake."

"But according to the map," Frank said, "his camp is nearby."

"And this should be part of his claim," Joe added.

"I'll go ahead and find the camp," Nancy suggested. "You two can ask those men if they've seen Jake or Rick."

Turn to page 76.

"I don't know . . ." Frank said hesitantly. "Maybe we'd better stay together and all go to the camp."

If you want to follow Nancy to the camp, turn to page 54.
If you want to follow Frank and Joe to the two men, turn to page 64.
If you think the three sleuths should stay together, turn to page 69.

Just then, their attention was caught by a soft scratching at the window. Nancy's worried face appeared, staring in at the three prisoners.

"Suddenly I feel a lot better!" Rick said and grinned at the pretty sleuth.

"But how can she get us out of here?" Joe asked nervously.

"Nancy will think of something!" Frank answered, but there was a worried edge in his voice.

"I wish she'd run away and get the police!" Rick said.

"I don't know, it may be too late for us by then," Joe added. "I hope she'll figure out a way to free us."

If you think Nancy should go to the police, turn to
page 97.
If you think she should try to rescue Rick and the
Hardys, turn to page 106.

"Nobody's here," he called softly after he reached the bottom. "Come on!"

But when Nancy descended the narrow stairs, they were startled to hear a voice whisper from a top bunk along the wall.

"You're wrong. Somebody is here. Am I glad to see you, Nancy!"

"Rick Jason!" Nancy gasped. "You almost scared me to death."

"Speaking of death, please get me out of here," Rick pleaded. "This place is like a coffin."

Nancy and Frank crept over to the bunk and found Rick tied to the mattress. The elder Hardy pulled a pocketknife from his jeans and cut the ropes.

"What's going on?" Nancy asked as they helped the reporter to the floor.

Just as Rick started to answer, they felt the boat lurch. It had been set loose from its moorings on the pier!

"Oh, no!" Frank gasped. "We're going out to sea!"

"Let's get off now!" Rick urged in a panicky voice.

Turn to page 79.

"That might be difficult," Frank declared. "Anyway, maybe we should stay here and find out where these guys are going."

If you think Nancy, Rick, and Frank should try to jump ship, turn to page 87.
If you think they should stay on board, turn to page 100.

"Rick went by canoe," Joe said. "I don't see why we shouldn't. We all know how to handle a boat."

"I'm with Joe," Frank added.

"Okay," Nancy agreed.

The Hardys flipped over the canoe, launched it into the water, and packed in the supplies they had brought from Fairbanks. Then Nancy stepped into the middle of the canoe, and the boys took up the paddles.

"Push off, Frank," Joe called out from the front of the boat. "This is going to be fun!"

The three sleuths were in high spirits as the canoe shot through the white water of the swollen river. The Hardys, who were experienced boatsmen, guided the small craft around large rocks and over rushing rapids.

"Look out!" Joe suddenly called. A short distance downriver, the rapids were dotted with threatening rough-edged stones.

Turn to page 81.

"This is going to be tricky!" Frank exclaimed as the canoe drifted closer to the rocks. "Hold on tight, Nancy!"

Turn to page 108.

"All right," the prospector grumbled reluctantly. "But we'd better hurry. Those two greenhorns won't stick around long to do the hard work it takes to find more gold. They may escape!"

Joe hoisted the heavy bag over his back, and Nancy led the way out of the tent. The two thieves did not see them as they crept into the woods.

Two hours later, they arrived at the Wiseman police station. Joe swung the heavy bag of gold down onto the ground, and slumped down beside it.

"Whew!" he sighed. "I don't think I'm cut out to be a prospector!"

After reporting the criminals, Nancy said, "We have a plane on the airstrip not far from town. Are you ready to go back to Fairbanks?"

"I sure am!" Rick answered. "Come on, Jake," he added. "You bring that gold along to Fairbanks and get the money you deserve."

"What about those nuggets in the river?" the prospector muttered. "I hope they'll still be there when I come back! All my life I've worked hard. Now I could be rich!"

Rick grinned "You will be," he said. "And what's more, I'll write you up in the paper!"

END

"I think Joe is right," Nancy said, examining the rough stones that slanted inward on the lighthouse wall. "He's a good enough climber to make it."

"Okay, you guys win," Frank agreed reluctantly. "But be careful, brother."

"Have I ever *not* been careful?" Joe asked in a teasing voice as he found his first foothold.

"Lots of times!" Frank answered with a worried sigh.

Frank and Nancy stared anxiously at the wall as Joe began to scale up to the window. He looked down once with a tense expression on his face, then continued his dangerous ascent.

"Thank goodness, he's made it!" Nancy whispered in relief when Joe hoisted his body through the dark opening. Then the younger Hardy disappeared from their sight.

"Let's take cover behind that rock," Nancy suggested, pulling Frank to a boulder near the lighthouse.

"I wonder what's going on?" Frank whispered nervously after ten minutes had passed. "Maybe we should knock on the door."

"Look!" Nancy exclaimed and pointed to the window through which Joe had disappeared.

Turn to page 85.

The two sleuths stared at the dark square and saw a rope being lowered from it. A moment later, Joe swung himself out of the opening and onto the rope.

"He's coming back," Frank said, as he and Nancy crept from their hiding place. "I wonder if he found anyone."

"Yes," Nancy said with a relieved smile. "Rick is right behind him!"

The two young men scrambled down the rope and dropped on the ground near Nancy and Frank.

"Nancy Drew!" Rick Jason exclaimed. "Are you a sight for sore eyes!"

Nancy gave him a quick hug, then asked anxiously, "Who's in that lighthouse?"

Turn to page 93.

86

"Let's go!" Joe insisted. "Perkins knows we're looking for Lyle Cooper. Maybe he'll lead us to him."

"Okay," Frank agreed as they made a quick dash to the rented Dodge.

The brothers jumped inside the old car. Frank revved the engine to life and took off after Dan Perkins.

"Good, we're still on his trail," Joe said as he sighted the brown van about half a mile ahead.

Frank accelerated until he had almost closed the distance between them.

"He's recognized us," Joe murmured as Perkins suddenly speeded up, "and he's trying to get away."

Frank continued to tail the man along the twisting mountain road. The van swung to the left onto a rutted dirt trail. The dark-haired detective managed to turn after it at the last minute.

"Watch out Frank!" Joe exclaimed. "He's braking to a stop."

Turn to page 114.

"Well, if we're going to jump, we'd better hurry," Frank called out as they heard the boat's engines roar to life. "I don't want to be caught and dumped into the Bering Sea!"

Nancy and Rick followed him up the stairs and through the hatch. Luckily, the two men at the bridge did not see them as they ran across the back end of the deck.

"It's going to be a cold swim!" Frank shuddered as he looked at the pier which was now about twenty yards away.

"Let's go for it!" Rick cried with a grimace and plunged into the choppy water. Nancy and Frank dived in after him.

"Swim fast!" Frank yelled, "before your bodies freeze up!"

Several minutes later, the three shivering investigators pulled themselves up on the pier.

"Wh-wh-where should we go first?" Nancy said through chattering teeth.

"The h-h-hotel," Frank answered. "We'll call the police and ch-ch-change clothes."

The friends made a run for the hotel, attracting curious stares from several Pribilof residents they passed.

Turn to page 88.

An hour later, they all sat in the lobby while Rick explained his story to the local authorities. Joe, who had investigated the lighthouse and found no one there, had joined them.

"The men who were holding me are planning an illegal seal kill at dawn tomorrow," Rick said. "They tried to recruit helpers among the natives here. One of them tipped me off about the hunt. Unfortunately, I was caught by those guys just before I was about to report them."

"Don't worry, we'll be waiting for them early tomorrow," the police chief said. "They won't get away with any seals."

Turn to page 96.

"Sh-sh-sh!" Frank suddenly whispered. "I think somebody's coming down right now."

The three immediately pressed their bodies against the lighthouse wall. They heard the old wooden door creak open and watched three men walk out. In the pale moonlight, the sleuths noticed that one of them had his hands tied behind his back.

"That's Rick!" Nancy said softly into Frank's ear as the men walked toward the beach.

"Look," Joe whispered excitedly and pointed to the water. "A boat is out there waiting for them."

"We have to help Rick escape!" Nancy urged.

"Don't worry," Joe whispered to Nancy. "Frank and I will sneak up and attack those two guys from behind. Wait for us here, though. This could get nasty."

Turn to page 90.

Nancy crouched in the shadow of the lighthouse, while Frank and Joe stealthily crept up to the three figures walking toward the water. The crashing of the waves against the shore covered any sounds the Hardys made as they neared Rick's captors.

Suddenly, Frank and Joe lunged forward and tackled the two thugs. Nancy watched the criminals crumble down onto the sandy beach, then she ran toward her friends.

Frank was untying the ropes around Rick's wrists.

"Nancy Drew! I can't believe it!" the reporter said in a dazed voice. "I thought I was a goner!"

"What happened, Rick?" the girl asked nervously.

"These men are spies," Rick replied, his voice edged with panic. "We've got to get out of here! Someone is coming to pick them up."

"That 'someone' is already here," Nancy told him, pointing to the boat lying in wait offshore.

"We can't leave these guys here!" Joe interrupted. "They'll get away."

"No they won't. I'm afraid we've knocked them out cold," Frank said. "We'll have to carry them back to the lighthouse. Then we'll barricade ourselves inside."

Turn to page 91.

Frank and Joe hoisted the two men over their shoulders and carried them into the abandoned building. Panting heavily, they dumped their captives on the floor, while Nancy and Rick bolted the door.

"We're safe now!" Rick gasped. "I know the rendezvous was supposed to be on the beach. That boat will leave if nobody is there to meet it."

"We'd better tie up those two guys before they regain consciousness," Frank cautioned. "I don't want to tangle with them again!"

"Here are the ropes they used on me," Rick offered.

"And as soon as the boat has left, I'll go for the police," Nancy suggested.

Turn to page 111.

After Dan Perkins had driven away, the two sleuths cautiously approached the small wood building. Frank tried the door, but found that it was securely locked.

"We've got to get in," Joe said with frustration. "I think we should try to break in."

Just then, the brothers heard a loud thump.

"Someone is in there!" Frank exclaimed.

The thumping continued, sounding like someone kicking an inside wall.

"Look at that window up there," Joe called out. "I could pry it open, if I could reach it."

"I'll help you," Frank offered and positioned himself underneath the window so that he could hoist his brother up.

Joe climbed onto Frank's shoulders and reached for the window. He pushed the pane up and peered inside.

"I think we've found who we're looking for!" he exclaimed. "I'm going in."

He slipped through the opening and dropped to the floor. A few minutes later, he opened the front door for Frank to enter the building.

Turn to page 95.

"Spies!" Rick answered. "And I'm lucky to be alive to write about them!"

"Rick was tied up in that room," Joe added. "His two captors are at the top of the lighthouse."

"I got a tip about a spy who was surveying the Alaskan defense system," Rick explained. "I followed him here to the Pribilofs, but he and an accomplice caught me. A submarine is supposed to surface any minute now some distance away from here. Another boat is coming to carry the spy out to it."

"I think we were on the boat you mean!" Nancy said. "How are we going to stop this?"

Frank had been deep in thought while he listened to Rick's story.

"I have a plan," he said. "We'll knock on the door to get the attention of the two guys inside. When they come out, Joe, Rick, and I will jump them. Then Nancy can run upstairs and turn on the big light. That keeps away anybody coming in from the sea."

"Okay, let's try it," Joe agreed.

Frank went to the lighthouse door and rapped on it. The sleuths anxiously waited as they heard footsteps approaching.

Turn to page 94.

As the door opened a crack, Frank leaped forward and pushed it open wide. The two men standing inside were taken by surprise and the Hardys and Rick jumped them and wrestled them to the ground. Meanwhile, Nancy ran up the stairs to the top of the lighthouse. She found the large spotlight and flicked a switch. A piercing beam shone out over the choppy sea!

I hope that'll do it, she thought as she hurried back down to help her friends bring the two men into town.

Turn to page 103.

"He fits Nancy's description of Rick Jason!" Joe said, pointing to a young man with reddish-blond hair and blue eyes lying on the floor, tied and gagged. Beside the reporter was a middle-aged man, also securely bound.

The two detectives worked to free the hostages, then introduced themselves. "We came up here with Nancy Drew to find you," Frank said to Rick. "What's going on?"

The young man cleared his throat and smiled gratefully at the Hardys.

"Lyle Cooper here tipped me off that a section of the pipeline near Livengood is in trouble. The contractor used inferior material and paid Dan Perkins to keep his mouth shut."

"I found out about the problem while working here," Lyle added. "I wanted a newspaper to report it. If those pipes aren't fixed, Alaska could have a big, ugly oil spill."

"How did you end up in this place?" Joe asked.

"Perkins caught us snooping around," Lyle explained. "He figured we were on to him."

"Let's get out of here!" Frank urged. "We'll pick up Nancy in Livengood and then head for the airport."

Turn to page 117.

At daybreak the next morning, Nancy, Frank, Joe, and Rick watched as the police apprehended the seal hunters on one of the island's broad beaches.

"I wish we could catch that guy who stole your Indian mask and my bag," Nancy murmured.

"Well, the mask was valuable," Rick added. "But it isn't as valuable as the lives of those animals."

Nancy walked closer to a young fur seal resting on the beach. It twitched its whiskers and stared at her with soft brown eyes.

"Good luck, little fellow," she said softly. "I hope you live a long, happy life."

END

On the other side of the window, Nancy Drew debated what she should do next. From a hiding place behind the outbuilding, she had watched Frank and Joe being captured by the mask thief and his accomplice. And now she knew that Rick was in the hands of the criminals as well.

I'd better go get help, she thought to herself. She gave the Hardys a signal with her hand, then crept away from the house, taking cover behind rocks and trees as she climbed up the hill again.

"This place is so desolate!" she said with a sigh as she reached the road. "Who knows when a car will come along!"

Then, to her relief, she noticed a vehicle approaching her from the direction of the town. As it drew near, she was happy to see that it was a police cruiser.

Nancy waved her arms wildly, and it braked to a stop beside her.

"Are you one of the people who came here from the airport?" the driver asked.

"Yes, and my friends have just been captured by two tough men in that house down there," Nancy said breathlessly.

Turn to page 98.

"Thank goodness that taxi driver stopped at the station to tell us about you," the second officer said. "He was worried about leaving you out here alone."

"Another friend of mine, a reporter from Anchorage, is in the house too," Nancy explained as she jumped in the back seat of the police car. "I think he was on the trail of a big story."

"We'll take care of those men," the driver promised as he turned off the main road, "You stay in the car. This could be dangerous."

They pulled up to the house, and the officers quickly jumped out of the car and rushed to the front door, their guns drawn. A moment later, they disappeared inside.

Nancy waited nervously, relieved that she didn't hear any gunfire. Several minutes later, the officers came back, pushing the two handcuffed criminals in front of them.

Nancy jumped out of the car and rushed into the house. She found Rick, Frank, and Joe still tied to the bedposts.

"Nancy Drew to the rescue!" Rick exclaimed with a grin. "Am I glad to see you!"

Turn to page 99.

"What is going on here?" Nancy asked, after she found a knife to cut the ropes that bound the three young men.

"One of the biggest gem-smuggling operations in the States!" Rick explained. "I'd been tipped off about it by an Anchorage jeweler. He had come into possession of a mask carved on this island that contained precious stones. I gave it to Rose Tutiakoff for safe-keeping."

"That mask was stolen from us at the airport by one of the criminals the police just arrested," Nancy explained. "He probably thought it still contained jewels."

"The smugglers brought the gems by boat from Asia to the Aleutians," Rick went on. "The stones were probably stolen there."

"I'm curious about the threatening call I took at your office about the seal kill," Joe said. "That's what brought us down here."

"The caller must have been someone on the Pribilof Islands. They don't like the stories I write against seal hunters."

Nancy shook her head in amazement.

"Rick," she said with a laugh, "now I know why you came to Alaska. It's certainly more exciting than River Heights!"

END

Frank climbed up the narrow stairs to peer out of the hatch. Just then the engine roared to life.

"It's too late to jump now," he called back softly. "We've pulled away from the dock."

He closed the hatch and joined Nancy and Rick again in the cramped sleeping quarters.

"What have you discovered, Rick?" Nancy asked tensely as the boat cut through the choppy sea.

"Several weeks ago," the reporter began, "I got a tip from a resident of the island that an illegal seal hunt was being planned. I flew here without telling anyone because I didn't want the story to break before I investigated it further."

"We picked up a threatening call at your office this morning," Frank explained. "That's what brought us down here."

"That must have been made just before I was captured," Rick replied. "I'd been staying with my contact here on the island. A clue led me to this boat, and I was caught snooping around."

"There's something else you should know, Rick," Nancy spoke up. "Rose Tutiakoff gave us a carved mask of yours. It was stolen at the Cold Bay Airport."

Turn to page 101.

"That mask was a valuable artifact," Rick said. "The thief must have known what he was stealing."

"Well, right now we've got a bigger problem," Frank muttered. "How many guys are on this boat?"

"Just two," Rick answered. "But they're planning a rendezvous with another boat tonight. They plan on killing as many seals as they can at dawn tomorrow."

"We've got to stop them!" Nancy exclaimed.

"Come on," Frank said with determination. "If we make a sneak attack, we can take over the boat!"

"I'm with you," Rick said.

"And I'll try to find the ship's radio," Nancy added. "If I do, I'll get in touch with the authorities on the island."

The group went up the narrow stairs onto the deck. As they crept to the front of the vessel, they spotted the two men in the wheel room.

"Ready, Rick?" Frank whispered.

"Ready!"

Turn to page 102.

The two young men charged at the criminals, taking them by surprise and wrestling them to the ground. Rick had brought along the ropes that he had been bound with, and he and Frank used them to tie up his captors. Nancy, meanwhile, disappeared through a door to the left.

"What are you doing here?" one of the men snarled.

"Saving the seals," Frank shot back.

"Look, Nancy found the radio," Rick exclaimed, pointing to a window through which they could see their friend using the ship's communication equipment.

Several minutes later, she joined them. "I contacted the authorities" she explained. "They're sending a boat out to meet us."

"Let's meet them halfway," Frank said with a grin. "I should be able to navigate this crate after all the practice I've had with the *Sleuth*."

Nancy joined him at the wheel.

"Well, Frank," she said. "Did you ever think you'd be sailing in the Bering Sea!"

Frank grinned. "Quite different from Barnet Bay, isn't it?"

Turn to page 113.

An hour later, the three young sleuths and Rick Jason sat in the local police station. The spy and his accomplice were locked securely behind bars.

"The lighthouse beam must have scared off the sub," Frank said. "It was violating the law of international waters and couldn't take the chance of coming in and being caught."

Rick nodded. "And I've got myself a big story, thanks to you guys!"

"There are still a few mysteries to clear up," Nancy interrupted. She went on to tell the reporter about the threatening phone call and about the stolen mask.

"I suspect," Rick said, "that the call was made by somebody who didn't want a seal kill publicized. I have written articles against it in the past. As for the mask, it's worth a lot of money. I hope to get it back!"

"Maybe we can help you," Joe said with a yawn. "But first I need a good night's sleep!"

END

"I haven't been in a good fight like that for a long time," Joe moaned, gingerly touching one swollen cheek.

"Good thing we knew more karate than those guys," Frank added.

"Here's some rope I brought along," the old prospector said with a satisfied smile. "We'll take care of them just like they took care of us."

By the time the men regained consciousness, they were securely tied up.

"That'll teach you to try to steal my gold," Jake muttered.

Rick and Nancy were talking a short distance away. The young reporter told her what had brought him up to the prospector's camp.

"I'm afraid Jake exaggerated a bit," he explained. "He said he was on to a big gold boom. This creek sure has a lot of nice nuggets in it, but it's not rich enough to make headlines."

"What's important is that you're safe," Nancy replied. "I have a private plane just outside Wiseman. Are you ready to go home?"

"Am I ever!" Rick exclaimed.

Turn to page 105.

Frank and Joe joined them.

"We'll march those two crooks back to Wiseman and contact the police," Frank said.

"I don't know about you," Joe announced, "but I'm eating something first. I'd trade all the gold in the world right now for one of the sandwiches in that backpack!"

END

Outside, Nancy carefully examined the window to the bedroom. She knew Rick and the Hardys were in big trouble.

She grasped the fishing knife she had found in the storage shed and slipped it under the window frame. To her relief, it moved upward as she turned the blade from side to side. Soon, there was enough space for her to put her fingers through the opening.

Nancy saw the tension on the Hardys' faces as she slowly pushed up the window. Frank coughed to cover the sound of the window creaking as it opened.

A moment later, Nancy hoisted herself up and dropped silently into the room.

Working quickly, she cut the ropes that bound her friends. As soon as they were free, all four crept to the open window and cautiously escaped from the house.

"Whew!" Joe whispered, "that was a tight spot we were in!"

"Let's get out of here!" Frank urged, leading the way back among the rocks and trees to the main road.

Turn to page 107.

"Those guys are part of a big smuggling ring," Rick explained once they were out of earshot of the house. "They receive stolen gems brought from Asia by boat. Then they ship the precious stones to Anchorage inside native masks made here. But how did you know where to find me?"

"We were on our way to the Pribilofs," Nancy replied. "Joe got a threatening phone call in your office which was meant for you. A man said to stay off the seal islands until after the kill."

"Really?" Rick said with surprise. "I might be missing a big story there! But you still haven't explained how you got here."

"Rose Tutiakoff gave us your mask and it was stolen during our stopover at Cold Bay. We followed the thief—and he led us here."

"He must have realized you were onto their scheme when he saw the mask," Rick reasoned. "I'd gotten it from a jeweler in Anchorage who suspected something illegal. We'd better tell the police all about this."

"It's going to be a long walk," Joe muttered.

"Maybe not!" Rick cried and pointed to a taxi swinging around a corner in the road. The driver was the same one who had brought the young detectives from the airport. He pulled up with a smile on his face.

Turn to page 119.

Together, Frank and Joe maneuvered the boat between the large rocks that stood at the head of the rapids. Then, with an exhilarating rush, the canoe shot through the broiling froth. Seconds later, the group was in calmer waters again.

"Frank, look over there!" Nancy suddenly exclaimed and pointed to the river bank on their right.

"Somebody didn't clear those rapids!" Frank yelled. "A canoe is broken up and caught in the tree roots."

The Hardys swiftly paddled over to the spot. When they reached it, they saw a figure collapsed on the long shore grass.

"I think it's Rick!" Nancy said in a worried voice.

An eerie howl pierced the air. The sleuths looked into the woods and spotted two timber wolves lying in wait.

"We got here just in time," Joe said grimly and jumped onto the shore. He waved his arms wildly over the body slumped on the bank. The two wolves ran off into the trees howling.

"Rick, are you all right?" Nancy said as she rushed up to the young man on the grass.

The reporter looked up into the blonde detective's face, his blue eyes dazed.

Turn to page 110.

"Nancy Drew?" he asked as though he were seeing a ghost.

"I came to find you," Nancy explained. "Frank and Joe Hardy are with me."

"My leg," the young reporter groaned, touching his right thigh. "I think it's broken."

"We have to get you out of here to a hospital," Frank said as he bent over Rick. "I'll hike back to Wiseman and call in a rescue plane. I don't want to chance those rapids again. Nancy, you and Joe stay here with Rick."

"Make it fast, brother," Joe said. "We have to be out of here by nightfall. Those wolves'll get even hungrier by then, and they'll probably be back."

As Frank ran off along the river bank, Nancy sat down next to her friend.

"What brought you here, Rick?" she asked softly.

"An old prospector named Jake," Rick explained. "He told me he had found a creek rich with gold not far from here. He claims it could be the start of another gold rush."

"Well," Nancy said with a smile, "that's one story you'll have to let go. I'm afraid you're in no shape to hike to Jake's cabin."

"No story," Rick agreed with a pained sigh, "and no amount of gold, would make me do this again!"

Turn to page 120.

Several hours later, Rick Jason and the young detectives were sitting in the hotel lobby, drinking big mugs of hot chocolate, going over the series of events that had taken place.

"You mean we actually caught a couple of international spies tonight?" Joe exclaimed.

"That's right," Rick answered. "I'd received a tip about them in Anchorage and followed them here to the seal islands. One of them caught me snooping around the lighthouse last night. I don't want to think about what they had planned for me," he added with a shudder.

"What puzzles me is that the call we picked up in your office had nothing to do with spies," Frank said. "I wonder what it was all about?"

"Apparently someone was staging a seal hunt and was afraid I'd publicize it," Rick replied. "There's so much controversy on that subject that people like to keep it quiet."

"I hope you'll get your valuable mask back," Nancy put in. "I'm sorry it was stolen."

"Listen, all I care about right now is being alive!" Rick exclaimed. "And I thank my lucky stars that you three came searching for me!"

END

Rick led the way to an open jeep parked across the street. They jumped inside and sped to the police station. On the way, Nancy explained that she had come to Alaska with Frank and Joe Hardy and that the brothers were following Dan Perkins.

A short time later, Nancy and Rick were sitting in the police station, and Rick had told his story.

"The pipeline is always in danger of sabotage," the police chief said as he buckled on his holster. "If those terrorists did manage to blow it up, the oil supply to the rest of the states could be interrupted for days."

"I can tell you where to find the evidence to convict those men," Rick said. "I made notes. They're in my room."

"Great. Now you stay right here," the policeman ordered, "until the arrest is over." He and two of his men left headquarters and roared down the road in a police cruiser with sirens blaring.

Turn to page 118.

A short time later, the young detectives were met by the police, and several officers boarded the commandeered boat. They continued on to intercept the unauthorized seal hunters. The criminals were apprehended and brought back to the island, where they were jailed.

The jubilant trio went back to their hotel for the night where they met Joe. He had investigated the lighthouse and, to his disappointment, had found no one there.

The next morning, Nancy, Rick, and the Hardys walked out to the rocky cliffs to see the seals.

"They're beautiful animals, aren't they?" Nancy murmured.

"And thanks to you, many of them have been saved," Rick added.

Just then, a chorus of barks erupted from the seals scattered across the rocks and beach.

"I think they just thanked us," Frank said with a broad smile.

END

Frank screeched to a halt behind the brown van. Joe jumped out as soon as he saw Dan Perkins open his door. Frank followed a moment later.

Perkins threw a worried look at the Hardys, then ran into the heavy trees by the side of the trail, with the boys in hot pursuit. Suddenly, Frank yelled, "The van, Joe! It's started to roll! Perkins must have left it in neutral."

He rushed back to the Dodge, jumped inside, and backed it out of the van's way. At the same time, his brother raced to the van and flung open the door on the driver's side. He managed to slide behind the wheel as the van picked up speed and started to careen downhill, out of control.

Joe jammed the brake to the floor, bringing the vehicle to a halt a few feet from a river ravine. He realized how close he had come to crashing down the steep incline and that his hands were shaking.

A moment later Frank ran up beside him. "Joe, are you okay?"

"I . . . think so." Joe pulled the emergency brake and climbed out of the van.

"Apparently you were thinking what I was thinking," Frank said as they walked around to the back of the vehicle.

Turn to page 115.

"I sure was," Joe replied. "I didn't risk my life just to save Perkins's van."

The younger Hardy opened the rear door.

"Look!" he cried out. Lying inside were two men with frightened expressions on their faces. Their wrists and ankles were bound.

"Rick Jason?" Frank asked the younger one with reddish-blond hair and blue eyes.

"That's me," the reporter answered. "But for awhile I thought I was a goner!"

"We're Frank and Joe Hardy, Nancy Drew's friends," Joe explained as he and Frank untied the two men. "Now you can tell us what kind of trouble you're in."

The young reporter scrambled out onto the ground and introduced his companion as Lyle Cooper.

"Lyle contacted me in Fairbanks about a faulty section of the pipeline," Rick explained. "If it isn't replaced, there could be a big oil spill that would damage the land and wildlife around here."

"Perkins was paid off by the supplier of the inferior materials," Lyle Cooper added. "He knew he would be in big trouble if we reported him, so he tried to keep us quiet."

Turn to page 116.

"The police will catch up with Perkins later," Joe said. "Right now, we'll take you back to Livengood. Nancy is there looking for you."

"I can't wait to see her," Rick said. "And thanks to both of you for saving us," he added, looking down into the ravine. "We were headed for a big spill ourselves!"

END

"Great!" Rick exclaimed as they ran out to the car. "I can't wait to see Nancy . . . and to thank her for saving my life!"

END

Later that afternoon, Rick, Nancy, and the Hardys met in the old hotel.

"All three terrorists are behind bars now," Nancy said with relief.

"When the police picked up Dan Perkins," Joe added, "they found dynamite in the back of his van."

"I have to call Matt Jenkins now," Rick said, getting up from his chair. "This story is so hot that the chief shouldn't mind that I disappeared for a while."

"One thing I'm sure of," Nancy added with a grin. "Alaska is lucky it missed this boom!"

END

"Need a ride?" he asked.

"To police headquarters, please," Nancy replied as they all piled into the cab. "And hurry!"

"As soon as we get there, I'm calling my bureau chief," Rick said. "This story is going to make headlines all over!"

END

Late that evening, Nancy, Frank, and Joe sat around Rick's bed in a Fairbanks hospital.

"How are you feeling now?" Nancy asked the young reporter, whose right leg was set in a cast.

"A lot better," Rick answered. "And a little foolish!"

Just then, Lisa Crawford appeared at the door.

"Hi Rick," she said with affection.

"Lisa!" Rick cried out, "How did you know . . ."

"Time for us to go," Frank declared and got up from his chair.

"We'll check on you tomorrow, Rick," Nancy added.

"Thanks, Nancy," Rick said softly. "Thanks for everything."

END

Here are some of the most recent titles in our exciting fiction series:

☐ Journey to Atlantis *J. J. Fortune* £1.75
☐ The Feud in the Chalet School
   Elinor M. Brent-Dyer £1.75
☐ Tomb of Nightmares *J. H. Brennan* £1.95
☐ The Emerald-Eyed Cat Mystery *Carolyn Keene* £1.75
☐ The Demon's Den *Franklin W. Dixon* £1.75
☐ The Mystery of the Kidnapped Whale
   Marc Brandel £1.75
☐ Horse of Fire *Patricia Leitch* £1.75
☐ The Garden of Madness *David Tant* 1.95

Armadas are available in bookshops and newsagents, but can also be ordered by post.

HOW TO ORDER
ARMADA BOOKS, Cash Sales Dept., GPO Box 29, Douglas, Isle of Man, British Isles. Please send purchase price plus 15p per book (maximum postal charge £3.00). Customers outside the UK also send purchase price plus 15p per book. Cheque, postal or money order — no currency.

NAME (Block letters) _____

ADDRESS _____

_____

_____